YOURS FOR CHRISTMAS

❄

ADDISON BLAIRE

YOURS FOR CHRISTMAS
A Christian Romance Novella
by Addison Blaire

Copyright ©2020 Addison Blaire
All rights reserved.

This is a work of fiction. Any resemblance to actual persons living or dead, businesses, events, or locales is purely coincidental or used fictitiously.

Reproduction in whole or part of this publication without express written consent is strictly prohibited. Do not upload or distribute anywhere.

This e-book is for your personal enjoyment only. It may not be resold or given away to others. Thank you for respecting the hard work of the author.

ABOUT

Her dreams were ripped away. He's mourning a crippling loss. Could a surprise reunion bring a Christmas miracle?

Essie Donovan is ready to move abroad to the mission field. Eager to share the good news in a foreign land, she's sold nearly everything she owns. But the morning of her flight, she learns that the person planning her trip took all the money and ran. Essie's left with only the luggage in her hands.

Noah Oakes has had the worst year of his life, losing both his parents and brother in a terrible accident. He's staying strong for the sake of his niece, who he's now raising in his brother's former home, but he doesn't see how either of them will have a good Christmas in the shadow of such a tragedy.

When a holiday gathering brings Essie and Noah together, neither can believe their eyes. It has been years since she turned down his marriage proposal. Though she still has feelings for him, Essie thinks running into him was only so she could make things right before leaving the country. Noah never stopped loving her, and he's determined to win the heart of the woman he's never been able to forget.

Is their faith strong enough to make their mismatched dreams come together, or does God have something else planned?

CONTENTS

Chapter 1 — 1
Chapter 2 — 6
Chapter 3 — 10
Chapter 4 — 14
Chapter 5 — 20
Chapter 6 — 26
Chapter 7 — 30
Chapter 8 — 35
Chapter 9 — 39
Chapter 10 — 44
Chapter 11 — 48
Chapter 12 — 53
Chapter 13 — 60
Chapter 14 — 66
Chapter 15 — 71
Chapter 16 — 76
Chapter 17 — 83
Chapter 18 — 86

Coming Soon — 89
Always You — 91

CHAPTER 1

Essie Donovan glanced over the empty apartment one last time before closing the door. She pulled her annoyingly long hair from her eyes and into a ponytail. Out of habit, she checked to make sure the door was locked before lugging her two stuffed suitcases and backpack down the flight of stairs. It was challenging because she couldn't lean on the railing, which was wrapped with garland and silver bulbs.

She stopped at the manager's office, where *Joy to the World* played over a speaker. Small white flakes floated outside the window.

Brianna gave her a sad smile as she took the manilla envelope and key from Essie. "I know you're going to have the time of your life, but Dylan and I will miss you."

That tugged on Essie's heartstrings. "I'll definitely miss you guys too."

Brianna laughed. "Right. You'll be too busy enjoying the warm beaches."

"You mean while I'll be busy laying the foundations for new houses."

"Still, I'm sure you won't have time to think of us."

She hesitated, needing to leave. Glanced at the clock—already five minutes late. But she let go of the luggage and raced around the desk and gave Brianna a big hug. "You'd better believe I'm going to miss you."

Her manager squeezed her tight. "You write, you hear?"

"Of course. It might take a while for the letter to get here."

"I'll wait."

"And give the kids my love." Essie hugged her again. "I wish you the best, and you guys will all be in my prayers."

"I appreciate it. The family moving into your apartment makes me nervous. I think that dad is going to give us trouble. It's going to be quite a year. Maybe you'll be back by then, when their lease is up? Then you can move back in, and I'll have a good reason to kick them out."

"Wish I could help you." Essie went back to her suitcases and opened the door. "I plan on staying in Guatemala for five years."

"Things could change, you know. Anyway, good luck with everything!" Brianna waved.

Essie pulled the bags out into the hallway and through the main doors. An icy breeze blew snowflakes in her face, making her shiver. She might actually miss the cold weather while on the mission field, but for now, she couldn't wait to get away from it.

The clouds looked dark, indicating a heavier snowfall could be on the horizon. Hopefully that wouldn't get in the way of her plane taking off. A plane that she needed to be on.

She hurried down the street, checking the time once more. Still behind schedule, but she would only miss Pastor Rick going over the itinerary *again*.

Essie already had it memorized. This mission trip was the dream of a lifetime. Growing up, she'd gone on countless similar trips with her family. None were nearly so long, and that was part of what made her blood rush with excitement, warming her despite the early December chill.

She turned the corner. Only another block before she reached the church. From her angle, she could already see the half a dozen cars in the parking lot.

Her pulse thrummed in her ears at the thought of stepping off the plane onto foreign soil and feeling the *warm* breeze before meeting the locals. After getting settled into her new home—a place barely a step above a shack based on the pictures—she would meet Daniela.

The sweet little girl's face appeared in her mind, sending a fresh wave of excitement through her. Weeks ago, the adoption had been finalized. She and Essie were going to be a family, and that little girl who only knew the life of an orphanage would have someone to love her every day.

She just hoped her Spanish lessons were enough to make communication successful. There would probably be blunders, but they would get by. She would be fluent soon enough being immersed in it.

Essie picked up her pace as soon as she reached the church parking lot. It was a struggle to get the wheels on the suitcases to keep up with her new speed. They bounced on rocks, and the luggage wobbled. But none of it mattered.

Soon she'd be in Guatemala!

Essie flung open the doors and rushed inside the large entry.

The defeat in the air was enough to suck the breath from her lungs. Tear-stained faces greeted her.

She dropped her bags, fearing that one of the older members had passed away. "What's the matter? It wasn't Bob, was it?"

Scarlett trudged over, wiping her eyes. "Nobody died, but—"

"That's great news." Relief washed through Essie. Bob had been in and out of the hospital, so she had been sure it was him.

Scarlett, the church's administrator, put her arm around Essie. "I'm sorry, sweetie. Your trip has been canceled."

A chill ran through her that had nothing to do with the winter temperatures outside. "Canceled? What do you mean?"

"Sarah is going to explain now that we're all here." Wiping her eyes, Scarlett led her to where the pastor's wife was talking with the rest of the missionary team.

"Let's sit in the sanctuary." Sarah motioned toward the open doors.

Essie's stomach churned acid and she came closer to throwing up with each step she took. The trip couldn't be canceled. Scarlett had to be mistaken.

But given all the downcast faces in the room, they were all upset. Maybe all of them were mistaken. They'd done everything they were supposed to. Gotten shots, filled out the paperwork, done fundraisers, prayed a thousand times.

There had to be some other explanation. The airplane would be leaving in three hours—the tickets had been paid for and the seats booked.

Everything was set. Tomorrow she would meet Daniela, and they would make a home together as a brand new mother and daughter team.

She could hardly focus as Sarah explained the situation. But from what she picked up, Norma, who had been heading the entire trip, had taken the money and run.

Not only was the trip off, but Essie's life savings was gone. She was stuck in the US with only the items and clothes in her three bags.

With nowhere to live.

No way to get to her adopted daughter who was expecting her.

The team members exchanged tearful embraces, and the room cleared one person at a time.

Essie sat glued to the pew, staring at the ornately carved cross hanging behind the pulpit.

How could this happen?

An arm wrapped around her shoulders. "Are you ready to

leave, sweetie?" Scarlett asked. "I'm sorry, but I need to lock the building. I have a family dinner I have to get ready for."

Essie swallowed, choking back a sob. "I have nowhere to go."

"What do you mean?" Scarlett's eyes filled with concern.

"I just turned in the key to my apartment. All of my money went into this. I wasn't just going to stay for the week, like everyone else. I'm moving there. Guatemala's my home for the next five years. Maybe longer."

Scarlett's mouth gaped. "That's right. I forgot, I'm so sorry."

"And now I can't get to the little girl I'm adopting."

"We'll talk to Pastor Rick about getting you down there some other way. I'll start a fundraiser myself if I have to. But for now, why don't you come home with me? I can't offer more than a couch, but at least it's a place to lay your head."

Tears blurred Essie's vision. "Okay, thanks."

"Let me help you with those suitcases."

Essie could hardly think as she followed Scarlett to her minivan.

All of her dreams had been smashed.

CHAPTER 2

Noah Oakes opened another drawer in the massive kitchen, still unable to find the turkey baster. He could never find what he was looking for in the enormous house.

His friends would laugh at him. They thought he was crazy for wishing he had his condo back when he had more than four-thousand square feet and ten acres to call home.

Not only did he find the space frustrating, the reason for moving in made him sick to his stomach every time he thought about it.

He'd give anything to go back in time and somehow change the horrible event that took place seven months and four days earlier.

Eight-year-old Abby wandered in and plunked onto a stool at the island, watching as Noah dug through another drawer. "Tell me again why we're having Christmas dinner now, when it's like a month away."

"Three and a half weeks," Noah corrected. He forced a smile, trying to get in the holiday spirit for her sake. "And it's because this is the only night everyone could make it. Besides, that gives us a chance to celebrate twice." He opened another drawer. "Did you turn on the outside Christmas lights?"

"It isn't dark yet." Abby pointed to one of the many windows.

"Won't be long." He turned back to the food. Any other day, he'd stop to take in the view of the trees and mountains behind them, now all snowcapped. His brother sure knew where to place the windows when he had this house built.

"Okay." Abby let out a long, drawn-out sigh.

Noah pushed aside his own heartache and pulled his niece into his arms. "I know how hard this is. I'm not sure how I'm going to get through Christmas either."

She looked up at him, tears shining in her eyes. "We're both having our first Christmases without our parents."

The lump in his throat reappeared. He nodded, blinking back tears. It only took one moment to take the lives of his parents, older brother, and sister-in-law. Now he and Abby had to figure out life without them.

Noah cleared his throat. "They wouldn't want us being sad today."

She wiped her eyes. "I guess."

He patted her back. "Go turn on the lights and some festive music. I've got to get that turkey out of the oven. Not sure why I agreed to prepare it—I've never made one before. It's probably burned or undercooked."

"It smells good." She sniffed the air before plodding out of the room, her shoes echoing on the hardwood floor.

Noah watched her, an overwhelming sense of grief seizing him again. While he hated losing his parents so young—he wasn't even thirty yet—it was so much worse for Abby. She'd only been seven at the time of the accident, and lost not only her parents but her grandparents too.

His mind wandered back to Christmases past. The times when he was about Abby's age were the best of memories. He'd looked at Adam with stars in his eyes, not thinking that his big brother was capable of doing anything wrong. He certainly never imagined life could be so cruel as to take him away so young.

Away in a Manger played from the other room, pulling Noah from his thoughts. He pulled out the turkey and checked the temperature. Perfect. It took some maneuvering to set the thing on the counter without dropping it. He hadn't been sure what size to get, so he picked the biggest one at the store, figuring everyone loved leftovers.

Ding-dong!

"I'll get it," Abby called.

"Thanks!" He checked the turkey. Thankfully, everyone coming was bringing the rest of the food, so he didn't have to worry about anything else. The bird was more than enough, and next year he'd ask one of his cousins to take charge of that. Scarlett would probably enjoy the task.

Ding-dong!

Excited conversation drifted from the hall.

Noah mumbled to himself. He should've put the turkey in sooner, but he'd gotten distracted walking by Adam and Cora's room. Despite the months that had gone by, neither he nor Abby had gotten the nerve to go inside. Noah had made one of the guest rooms his, refusing to touch his brother's things.

Ding-dong!

Now everyone was here. He shoved aside thoughts of family members who wouldn't make the dinner and forced a smile as he greeted his relatives. Though the atmosphere was festive, it also held sadness. Nobody was talking about his parents or Abby's, but their absence couldn't be ignored.

Scarlett directed her four kids to the living room and pulled Noah aside. "I tried calling you, but you didn't answer."

"I was running around like a chicken with my head cut off. This was the wrong year to attempt the turkey."

She gave him a playful shove. "I told you I could cook it."

"And I should've listened. What were you calling about? Everything okay?"

"Yes, no worries. I just have a guest. Hopefully that's okay."

"It's fine. You could bring four more kids, and there'd still be too much turkey."

Scarlett laughed. "Just one. She goes to my church, and is currently staying on my couch because she's having a rough time."

"I can certainly relate to that." He sighed.

"It must be so hard on you and Abby. It kills me, and I wasn't nearly as close to any of them."

"Thanks. Why don't you introduce me to your guest?"

Scarlett gave him a quick hug before leading him into the busy living room. Kids were jumping around and adults were grouped together, talking and laughing.

His cousin tapped the shoulder of someone in an emerald green dress and long dark hair that went almost to her waist.

The woman turned around, her sad green eyes widening as her gaze met his.

He knew those eyes.

Noah had spent hours memorizing them. But that had been a lifetime ago.

Essie was even more beautiful now than the day she'd refused his marriage proposal.

The last time he'd seen her.

His breath caught, and he was only vaguely aware of Scarlett talking.

Her face flushed red and she stepped back, looking around. For an escape, no doubt.

Noah's heart hammered.

How was he going to get through the meal with her here?

CHAPTER 3

❄

Essie pretended to take another bite of turkey. Hopefully nobody noticed her pushing the food around her plate. She could hardly eat with Noah at the table.

Her mind swirled, trying to make sense of the situation. How had he made enough money to afford such a large, beautiful place? When had he gotten married? Abby was obviously his—they had the same big chocolatey eyes and dusting of freckles underneath. She couldn't be younger than seven or eight, so he had to have turned around and found someone right after they broke up.

She'd meant that much to him.

It had killed her to say no to his proposal. She'd always thought it had crushed him too. He'd put so much thought into it, taking her to their favorite beach and setting up a picnic. It had been their most romantic date, and given the amount of flowers around the blanket, she should've seen it coming.

But she hadn't. Marriage had been the furthest thing from her mind—and it still was. Her parents had just invited her on a mission trip to Romania and she was going to break up with

Noah that week because it wouldn't be fair to ask him to wait eighteen months for her return.

The timing couldn't have been worse. She'd had no idea he was thinking about getting engaged. Her only thoughts were of serving and sharing the good news with the orphans halfway across the world. Noah had just accepted a job and bought a condo.

They were living in two completely separate worlds. And they continued to be, maybe more so now than ever.

Essie pushed her thoughts aside and looked around the table. She still hadn't been able to figure out who Noah's wife was. He hadn't held anyone's hand or given a kiss to anyone. To make it even more confusing, he sat between Abby and one of his uncles, Scarlett's dad.

People started clearing their plates and talking about a cherry pie someone had stuck in the oven.

Essie quickly put her napkin on her plate to hide the fact that she'd only picked at her food. She made small talk with people whose names she couldn't remember and others she hadn't seen in years—there were so many people in this family—and then made her way to the living room for some air.

The kids filtered in, laughing loudly and playing around. Under any other circumstance, she'd have happily engaged them in conversation, but this night she didn't have it in her.

She tiptoed down a hall and crept into a sitting room. Though music and conversation sounded, it was much quieter. It helped her to relax.

Essie wandered the room, taking in the framed photos. There were a lot more pictures of Adam and a gorgeous blonde with Abby than there were of Noah with the girl.

Had she gotten it wrong? Was Noah Abby's uncle? But why weren't Adam and the blonde here? If Abby was their daughter, and they were on vacation, she would be with them and not here. Another thing didn't make sense. Why did everyone act like this place was Noah's?

It was all so confusing.

Not that it mattered. As soon as Scarlett was ready to leave, Essie would never have to see or think about Noah again.

She needed to figure out how to get to Guatemala. How to get ahold of the adoption agency and let them know what had happened. Poor Daniela still thought Essie would be arriving to pick her up and take her to their new home tomorrow.

Sighing, she collapsed onto the couch and stared out the window. Little white flakes floated down, shining red, blue, and green as they reflected the outside lights.

If only she could talk to her mom, but her parents were unreachable. Their current mission field was a tribe in Africa where the nearest phone was an hour's drive and there was no cell service. She'd also love to speak with Hannah or Jacob, but her brother and sister were on their own mission trips with their families.

She was the only one still in the states. The only one not serving the poor. Instead, she was sitting in an enormous house, wearing an expensive dress. She tugged on the hem, finding it too short while she sat. If it had been her choice, she'd have worn something completely different. But she didn't have a holiday dress, and this was what Scarlett offered her. She was lucky it fit, as did the shoes. They were a tad snug, but she and Scarlett were so close in size.

Although if she had nothing acceptable to wear, she wouldn't have had to come to this party in the first place. What were the chances that Noah would be here? She'd had no clue that Scarlett and Noah were related. But Scarlett had only recently moved to the area, so Essie had never had the chance to meet her when she was dating Noah.

Footsteps sounded down the hall.

Essie looked for a place to hide. Nothing. Not without

crouching behind the sofa and making the dress rise up even higher than it was now.

Noah stepped into the doorway. His dark hair fell slightly over his eyes. He brushed it away but otherwise didn't budge, his gaze on her. Other than being slightly broader and having a little longer hair, he looked just like he did before.

And he looked *at* her just like before.

It made her pulse race. That hadn't changed either.

Essie swallowed and rose, adjusting the strange dress. Tried to think of something to say. But what could she say to the person she'd loved and walked away from him at his most vulnerable moment?

There was no escape. Noah took up the entire doorway.

She needed to face her most shameful moment. She'd been running, and this was why God had brought them together. Maybe even why her move to Guatemala had been stalled.

It was time to right a wrong before moving to her next step in life. And she had better get it right before her plans were put on hold again.

She cleared her throat. "Noah."

Her palms grew sweaty. What would he say?

Could he possibly forgive the selfish and rash way she'd treated him?

CHAPTER 4

Noah's heart pounded. He drew a deep breath and leaned against the wall for support. It wasn't the time to let on that she made him weak in the knees. Literally.

How was it Essie had managed to grow even more beautiful and graceful? He'd already thought she was the most beautiful woman in all of creation back when he'd had the pleasure of being her boyfriend.

He realized he hadn't yet responded to her. She'd said his name. It never sounded better than when it came from her lips. Almost like a choir of angels singing praises.

Noah cleared his throat. "It's good to see you again, Essie."

Her eyes widened slightly. "Is it?"

Oh, those eyes. He'd always thought *those* were the pinnacle of creation. Though he wasn't much of a romantic, she turned him into one just by being close.

He stepped into the room slowly, careful not to show that his knees could give out at any moment. "I've missed you."

She dropped her gaze, her long lashes covering her eyes. "How can you say that?"

"Because you were the woman I wanted to marry."

Her eyes snapped back up at him at the word wanted. Past tense.

The space between them felt thick as water, like moving closer to her would be fighting the ocean.

"Why'd you run off without explanation?" A lump formed in his throat. "I'd have accepted a no. If it wasn't the right time, I'd have waited."

She stepped away from and twisted her long hair around a finger. "I'm really sorry for the immature way I handled it. Your proposal made me realize some things, and I didn't know how to respond at the time."

"Realize what?"

"That we had different goals and dreams."

"Now, that's not true."

Her head tilted. "What do you mean?"

"Can we sit?"

Essie hesitated but did sit, and continued playing with her hair.

He took the cushion next to her, leaving more space between them than he wanted. It was close enough that he could smell her perfume—a different one but still with the sweet citrus she'd always liked. "What makes you think we had different dreams?"

Her gaze flitted back and forth, and the depth of her eyes showed confliction. "Isn't it obvious?"

Noah shook his head no, resisting the temptation to take her hand and offer comfort. It felt so right being in her presence, but it had been so long. Things had changed.

He'd changed.

But neither of them had a wedding band. There was still hope.

However, he didn't want to risk his heart breaking all over again. It wasn't something he could live through. Not so close to losing his parents and brother.

Essie leaned back and sighed. "All I've ever wanted was to be on the mission field."

"I've never been opposed to that. Remember me saying I wanted to go with you on one?"

She frowned. "That's exactly it."

"I don't follow."

Essie glanced up for a moment. Perhaps praying for the right words. She turned to him, a sadness in her eyes that once again urged him to comfort her.

But it wasn't appropriate. They were practically strangers now, despite how he felt in her presence.

She crossed one leg over the other. "For me, the mission field is a lifestyle. I grew up going on long-term trips. Not the week-long ones that are so popular."

He nodded. "I know."

"How would that ever work? You wanted your career and I was getting ready to leave for Romania."

"I'd have waited for you. Once we were married, I'd have followed you to the ends of the earth."

Her mouth gaped. "But your career …"

"Never held a candle to you. That's why I couldn't understand your walking away so easily."

"It wasn't easy—it was the hardest thing I've ever done." She took a deep breath. "And I've always regretted the way I handled it. It wasn't fair to you, and I'm truly sorry. I hope you can find it in your heart to forgive me someday."

"Already done."

"Really?"

"Of course."

Her expression was unreadable. Was she relieved? Surprised? Or thinking something else altogether?

Silence rested between them.

He leaned back. "Have you been on any mission trips lately?"

She frowned and looked away.

"Is that a no?"

Essie's lips wavered and she turned her attention to a nail. "I should be on a plane to Guatemala right now."

Now he really wanted to pull her into his arms. "Why aren't you?"

"The person in charge took the money and ran. All of my money went to the trip. I don't have the funds to get another ticket."

Anger burned in his chest. "That's horrible! What are you going to do now?"

She shrugged. "I'm still taking it in. The pastor's wife is looking into the next steps—maybe finding Norma and trying to get the money back. Scarlett says she'll start a new fundraiser. I know God has a plan, but I don't know what it is."

Noah couldn't take it any longer. He rested his hand on top of hers. "If I can do anything, let me know."

"I couldn't ask anything of you."

"I'm offering."

She pulled her hand away and wiped her eyes. "You can pray for me. It's such a shock, and I'm left with just three bags of my belongings."

"What do you mean?"

"I sold everything for the trip." Her voice cracked. "I turned in the keys to my apartment this morning, my position at work has been filled, and I'm staying on Scarlett's couch until I can find a way down there."

"What about your parents? Or Hannah or Jacob?"

"They're all on their own mission fields. And what's worse, the little girl I'm adopting is expecting me tomorrow. Daniela's going to be so confused and disappointed."

"You're adopting?"

Essie nodded. "I'm going to be spending the next five years down there. Well, I was. I'm not sure what's going to happen now."

She looked more deflated than a torn balloon.

"I'm so sorry." He pulled her into an embrace and rubbed her back. They fit like a glove, like always. "I can't imagine how awful you must feel."

Essie didn't resist. She didn't put her arms around him either.

"I'm serious about my offer to help. If you need a place to stay, there's a guesthouse just past the horse stables. It's on the dusty side, but you'd have it to yourself. I can't imagine staying on Scarlett's couch will offer much privacy in a house with six other people."

She sat up straight and pulled hair from her eyes. "I appreciate the offer, but I can't."

"It's a whole separate building that never gets used. You wouldn't be putting me out, if that's what you're worried about."

"I couldn't pay you rent."

"Doesn't matter, because I wouldn't take it if you tried to pay me."

"Thanks, but I'll stay at Scarlett's. I'll be able to find a new job until this mess gets sorted."

"My offer stands."

Laughter roared from the other room.

"We should get back to the party." He rose and offered his hand.

She placed her hand in his. It was so soft and smooth, and it felt so right in his as he helped her up.

"What about you?" She asked. "Do you live here with Adam?"

Noah flicked his gaze to a picture of his brother beaming as he held newborn Abby at the hospital. "No. He and his wife, along with our parents, all died seven months ago. They left everything to me, including Abby."

Essie covered her mouth. "That's heartbreaking. I'm so sorry."

"I appreciate it. It's been the most challenging year."

"And here I've been complaining about my canceled move while you've been dealing with that."

"Don't compare griefs. We're all given our own heartaches, and as long as we turn them over to God, he'll turn them into blessings. Even if it seems impossible in the middle of the storm."

She nodded. "May I ask what happened? The accident?"

"It was a plane crash."

"Seven months ago? That one that went down in the Nevada desert?"

"Yeah." Noah closed his eyes, images from the evening news spinning in his mind. No matter how hard he tried to forget the sight, they were seared into his memory. He was just grateful Abby had been spared seeing them.

Essie put her hand on his arm. "That was all over the news."

He nodded, not trusting his voice. His pain was all the more raw with her standing so close.

"It struck me so hard," she said. "I've been praying for the victims' loved ones since I first heard about it. I had no idea I was praying for you."

And she also had no idea he'd been praying for her all these years. She wouldn't know either, because he wasn't going to tell her. The best thing he could do for her would be to help her get to Guatemala to unite her with her adopted daughter.

If she'd accept his help.

CHAPTER 5

A plastic ball bounced off the back of Essie's head. She turned to see little Connor, his mouth wide open.

"Sorry, Miss Essie!"

She smiled. "It's okay. Just be careful you don't break any of your mom's lamps or vases."

"I won't." He grabbed his ball and ran from the room.

Essie turned back to her phone and scrolled through the job listings. There wasn't anything that was really a match.

Music blared from another room.

It was also hard to think in this house. She'd grown up in a home with three kids, but it wasn't half as noisy as Scarlett's home with four.

Darcy, the golden retriever, ran past, followed by the two youngest kids. They laughed and shrieked as they chased after the poor dog.

Essie sighed. She'd have an easier time trying to find a job while sitting in a movie theater during a loud action scene.

That wasn't a half-bad idea. Not that she would try it, but getting out of the house would do her some good. Maybe there was a quiet coffee shop nearby or even a park. With snow trickling down and sticking to the grass, people would likely be staying inside.

She grabbed her jacket and purse then found Scarlett. "I'm going to get some fresh air."

"It's a little loud in here, isn't it?"

Essie forced a smile. "Just a little. I'd like to find a job so I can get out of your hair."

"You're no bother. Stay until the trip is rescheduled."

"Thanks." She stepped outside, barely dodging another of Connor's flying toys.

The street in front of Scarlett's house was quiet, but a block down was a main road. It was filled with people, many carrying shopping bags no doubt filled with Christmas gifts for loved ones.

Her heart ached at the thought. Not that her family had ever been one to go overboard with gifts—not with three kids and spending so much time and money on the mission field—but she missed the time spent together. Now they were spread across the world. Perhaps next year they could all meet for the holiday.

Essie pulled her hood up and zipped the coat as high as it would go. She hurried toward the main street and looked for a coffee shop. After buying a calming chamomile tea with the last of her last cash, she settled into a chair and scrolled through more job listings.

Someone bumped her arm.

Essie let go of her cup. Watched in horror as it bounced on her lap in slow motion. She reached for it, but the lid came loose. Hot tea spilled all over her jeans and down on the floor. She leaped up and set down her now-empty drink.

"I'm so sorry!" The woman looked like she meant it. "I'll grab you some napkins." She ran off before Essie could respond. Once she arrived, the two of them wiped the floor, the other lady apologizing nonstop. "Let me buy you another drink."

"No, it's okay. Really." Essie wiped her pants which had gone from hot to cold.

"I feel so bad."

"Don't. Accidents happen. I'm fine."

But the woman came back with a spiced apple cider drink that had to have cost at least twice what the tea had. She also shoved a gift card in her hand.

"I can't take this," Essie said.

"Sure you can. I just ruined your day, and I feel awful. Merry Christmas." She darted out of the coffee shop before Essie could return the card.

Essie sat back down, exhausted.

Some boys ran by and laughed at her.

The spilled tea made it look like she'd wet herself.

Sighing, Essie dragged herself into the bathroom. Something was finally going her way—there was a hand dryer next to the sink. She stood under the warm air until her pants dried. They were a little stiff, but at least no longer looked bad.

Now every chair was taken. So much for a quiet place to look into job opportunities.

Maybe a prayer walk was what she needed. At least her clothes were no longer soaked.

She sipped the cider as she strolled down the busy street, careful to avoid puddles. The snow wasn't sticking to the pavement, but it was melting like crazy.

Essie glanced up at the dark gray clouds, blinking quickly as white flakes floated down. "I'm sorry, Lord, that I didn't think to pray about this first thing in the morning. Instead, I jumped right into the job search without seeking what you'd have me do."

The image of the little guesthouse on the other side of Noah's horse stables popped into her mind.

"Well, I know *that* isn't your will." She had made her peace with him, and now it was time to move on.

Essie shoved the images from her mind and continued on, looking for a quieter prayer spot. Maybe a bench on a side street or in a park.

As she passed a bakery with aromas that made her mouth water, she saw a little park beyond the alleyway. The perfect place.

Honk! Honk!

She turned toward the cars just as a sports car ran through an enormous puddle. It splashed mud and water all over her. Mud stuck to her face and eyelashes. Clung to her hand, and even got on the lid to her cider.

"What are you trying to tell me, Lord?" She dumped her second drink into the nearest garbage bin and wiped as much mud off as she could.

Blinking back tears, she hurried through the alleyway over to the bench and sat on it.

Why was all of this happening? What was the message God was trying to tell her?

If only he would speak audibly. That would make things so much easier. But that wasn't the way things worked.

The guesthouse appeared in her mind again.

"Is that what you're trying to tell me? That can't be right. Not him, not now. Not ever, actually."

It appeared again, but this time with the added image of her walking up to it with her three bags in hand.

Essie raked her hands through her hair, mud getting stuck under her nails.

At least his guesthouse would be quiet. Nobody would bump into her or get her wet.

She glanced up at the sky again. "Okay, I'll call the number I have for Noah. If it still goes to his cell phone, then I'll take it to mean you want me to ask about staying there. If not, I'll assume it's just a temptation I should ignore."

Hands shaking, she found his number in her contact list.

Would it go to him? Or would someone else answer?

There was only one way to find out. Her thumb hovered over the call button for a moment before she pressed it.

It rang.

She nearly ended the call.

Someone answered mid-ring.

Her breath caught.

"Essie?"

A warmth spread through her at hearing Noah's voice.

"Are you there? Hello?"

"I ... I'm here. I wasn't sure this was still your number."

He laughed—another sound that sent a wave of warmth. "It hasn't changed. How are you?"

She brushed more mud off her pants. "I'm wondering if your offer is still open. You know, for your guesthouse. I just need a quiet place to look for a job. Like I said, I'll pay you rent."

There was a pause.

Her heart raced. Maybe she shouldn't have asked. It was dumb. He'd probably changed his mind. Probably thought she was crazy. Or mean. She'd left him after he proposed, after all.

"Move in any time," Noah said finally. "But I won't take your money. Save it for your mission."

"I can't—"

"Actually, I have a proposition for you."

"What do you mean?" she asked.

"It would help me out a *lot* if you could take care of the horses for me. In fact, I'd pay you for your time. I've been thinking about selling them, but the thought brings Abby to tears. However, the fact of the matter is, I don't have time for them."

Essie stared in disbelief at the building in front of her. "You want to *pay* me to stay in your guesthouse?"

"No. To take care of the horses."

"I do love horses."

"I know. What do you say?"

She glanced up at the sky and down to her muddy jeans and coat.

The answer seemed clear.

"Yes, I'll help you with the horses."

"Great." It sounded like he was smiling. "I'll be by Scarlett's in an hour to pick you up."

CHAPTER 6

Noah closed the stable doors behind them. "Still up for the job?"

Essie's smile lit up her face. "It won't even feel like work. I've missed being around horses so much, but didn't realize it until just now."

His heart warmed. "Perfect. The guesthouse has everything you need, but you're more than welcome to join Abby and me for meals. Or I can stock your fridge. It's up to you."

"I couldn't ask—"

"You aren't asking."

The slightest shade of pink colored her cheeks. "I appreciate the offer, but I don't want to take advantage of your generosity."

"Have you seen this place? I can afford to be generous, thanks to my brother. Before this, I lived in a condo, which was really just a glorified apartment."

She smiled, and her expression brought him back to a time when they were volunteering at a homeless shelter together. She'd had that same look when serving the needy.

He cleared his throat. "I don't want you to think that I'm more than I am—or worse, that I *think* I'm more than I am. It was my brother; he's the one who earned all of this stuff. I just inherited it to take care of his girl."

"That's like all of us." She looked deep in thought for a moment. "What do we have that God hasn't given to us?"

The depth of her insight struck him. "I never thought of it that way. At any rate, what I have is yours while you're here. If you're hungry, raid my fridge. If something in the guesthouse isn't working, then find what you need in the main house."

"Thanks again for everything." She pulled her gaze away and wandered over to the nearest horse, petting her on the nose and speaking softly.

Noah took advantage of the moment to take her in. She was really in her element out here and didn't seem to notice the cold, whereas he was already looking forward to splitting some wood to start a fire.

Essie moved to another horse, petting and talking to him.

It still hardly seemed possible that she was back in his life. Yet here she was, now living on the same property with only a horse stable between them.

His pulse sped up. Could this be a second chance at love? It wasn't like Noah hadn't dated others in the years between, but nobody ever measured up to Essie. How could they? She was not only beautiful but also selfless. Even now, homeless and with all of her money stolen, all she could think about was not taking advantage of him, and also of a little Guatemalan girl who was expecting her.

Most of the other women he'd dated in the interim would be throwing a fit by now. He hadn't heard her utter one complaint —no harsh words for the thief.

It was inspiring. Made him want to be a better man.

She'd always had that effect on him, even when he was young.

He leaned against the nearest wall and waited for Essie to

finish petting all the horses. The cold was bothering him less with every passing moment.

When she was done, Essie spun around, her eyes wide and a big smile on her face. "Thank you so much for letting me take care of them."

The woman was nothing short of amazing.

And she was waiting for a response.

Noah stepped away from the wall and regained control over his tied tongue. "I'm the one who should be thanking you. Do you need anything else? Dinner, maybe?"

She chewed on her lower lip. "That would be great. Will I have time to settle in first?"

"Take your time. It's nothing fancy. I'm warming up leftovers from the party. Hope you don't mind."

"It sounds great." She gave him a warm smile. "When should I make my way over?"

"Will an hour give you enough time to settle in?"

"I think so. Anything I can bring?"

"Just yourself." He pushed the door open, holding it until she went through, then closed and locked it.

"Will I need a key?" she asked. "Or will you be unlocking it every morning?"

He twisted it off his keyring. "You can have this one. There's another set inside for the gardener."

Essie lifted a brow.

"Yes, my brother hired a gardener. It wasn't my idea, but it sure saves me time. Someday I'd like to take a stab at some of it myself, but that day isn't today."

The corners of her mouth wobbled. "I'll see you in an hour, Noah."

His skin warmed hearing his name roll off her lips. He wanted to kiss those lips again soon. Preferably at an altar.

He quickly cleared his throat—and his mind. "Sounds great. I'll be waiting."

She gave him a curious look before spinning around and strolling back to the guesthouse where her three bags waited for her.

Noah released a breath he hadn't realized he was holding once the door closed behind her. He should be surprised at himself for thinking about marriage, but at the same time, it was impossible not to.

Essie Donovan was the only woman he'd ever wanted to wed. And he couldn't see that changing anytime soon.

Especially not now that she'd walked back into his life just as he was starting to overcome the heartache from losing most of his family earlier in the year. He would never forget them or stop missing them, but the pain was finally manageable most days. There were even times he could think about them with real joy.

But could he deal with the possibility of a wedding without his brother as his best man or his dad not officiating?

The air escaped his lungs.

It was just as well. The woman he had never stopped loving was planning on spending the next five years with a country between them.

Sadness blanketed him as he made his way to the woodpile to ready the fire. It was probably for the best if he just focused on Abby. Who knew how long Essie would stay? At least when she left he would have the knowledge that she hadn't walked away from him because she didn't care for him.

It was because their lives didn't align.

He'd be smart to simply enjoy the additional time with her.

Unfortunately, his heart rarely listened to his brain.

CHAPTER 7

Essie made sure she put everything back before stepping outside and locking the stable door. She breathed in the fresh air and took in what remained of the sunrise, feeling great from the night of uninterrupted sleep.

Snow from the night before crunched under her shoes as she made her way slowly back to the guesthouse, enjoying the scenery. The property was still in town, but far enough on the outskirts that it may as well have been out in the country. The woods surrounding it made the air so much cleaner than what she was used to breathing.

She hesitated at the door. As nice as the little building was, it didn't hold a candle to the outdoors. She tightened her now-clean jacket around her and headed around behind the stable, taking in the sight.

The tops of the pine trees were white, as were the mountains in the distance. It was breathtaking. Even though she was supposed to be in a warm, sunny place with a coastline of bright blue water—or at least that was how she pictured it. The climate wasn't why she wanted to go to Guatemala. It was the people.

She was eager to learn their culture and help them in ways that would open their hearts to the good news.

It still made no sense that she was here, although staring at the scenery before her gave her peace. Even though she didn't understand the circumstances, she was still in God's creation, able to appreciate his creativity. His love shone through all of nature, whether it be snow or blistering heat.

She pulled out her phone and looked at the pictures of Daniela that had been emailed to her by the adoption agency. In one she beamed, showing off a missing tooth. She had her arm around a little boy in another.

Essie returned the device to her pocket and prayed that the sweet little girl wasn't too disappointed about the delay—that she'd even gotten word about it. The last thing Essie wanted was for Daniela to think she'd changed her mind.

She squeezed her hands tightly and begged God to make sure Daniela got the message soon, if she hadn't already.

It broke her heart to think of what her future daughter could be thinking at that very moment.

Her phone buzzed in her pocket, startling her.

Essie pulled it out again and answered the call. It was her pastor's wife. "Sarah?"

"I'm glad I caught you, dear. I have some good news."

"Is the trip back on?" Essie's breath hitched in anticipation.

"No. I'm sorry. But Daniela's caregivers explained the situation to her, so she knows that you're still trying to get to her."

Essie breathed a sigh of relief and silently thanked God for the answered prayer. "That's such wonderful news. I was so worried."

"I know," Sarah said. "That's why I wanted to tell you right away."

"What about the mission trip? How soon can I get down there?"

"Unfortunately, Norma never set up anything. She was really

deceptive and sneaky—she'd been planning on running with the funds the whole time."

Tears stung her eyes. "How could that have happened?"

"Rick and I take full responsibility for that. We should've looked closer at what she was doing and not trusted her blindly. That will never happen again. We've learned our lesson."

"But what about going to Guatemala?"

"We're speaking with the staff about fundraisers. Some of our members have already donated after hearing about what happened. But we'll have to put together another team. Several of the people have already said they won't go on this next one."

"How could they not?"

"They're hurt. We all are, and everyone reacts differently. And you're the one with the strongest ties. Everybody else was only planning on staying for the week."

Essie frowned, looking to the heavens for comfort. "I was the only one planning on adopting and staying long-term."

"Yes. But I promise you that if nothing else, we'll get you down there."

Tears blurred her vision. "I appreciate it, Sarah. I really do."

"It's the least we could do. I've got to go, but I'll keep you updated."

They said their goodbyes, and Essie wiped her eyes. If only they could find Norma, get everyone's money back, and prosecute her to the full extent of the law.

Guilt stung for thinking such a vindictive thought. She should be praying for Norma's heart and repentance. She was clearly far from God, and that should be Essie's main concern.

She almost didn't care. But she would get there. It might take quite a lot of prayer, but she wouldn't let her heart harden.

Snap!

It sounded like a branch broke around the corner of the stable. Either a wild animal was close, or a person was.

Her heart leaped into her throat as she whipped around.

Maybe it was just the gardener Noah had mentioned.

Noah sauntered around the corner, an axe in hand and wood chips stuck to his hair and flannel jacket. He was also unshaven, and the entire look made her breath catch. She couldn't pull her gaze from him.

He set the tool down. "Didn't mean to surprise you. Just chopping more wood in case the power goes out."

"Is it supposed to?"

"They're calling for heavy snow tonight. I put some pieces outside the guesthouse door in case you want them. But you're also welcome to come to the house anytime."

Unable to find words, she just nodded.

He stepped closer, his eyes filling with concern. "Have you been crying?"

Essie's face flamed.

Noah brushed some hair from her face. "What's the matter?"

She looked away but then turned back to him. "I was just speaking with my pastor's wife. They're working on a new mission trip, but I can't help being upset about the way things worked out. I'm angry with the woman who tricked us all."

"Anyone would be."

"I need to forgive her."

He took her hand in his, swallowing it. "You also need time to process all your emotions."

"But I want her to pay! I want revenge. That isn't right."

Noah squeezed her hand. "What *she* did was wrong. It's normal to be furious. Don't fight it, but don't get stuck there either."

She studied his eyes, getting lost for a moment. "You speak from experience."

"For a while, I hated everyone responsible for that plane crash. It's never just one person's fault when something major like that happens. It's many people overlooking numerous red flags."

"You hated them?"

He frowned. "I did. In fact, I'm glad God didn't bring you back into my life then. You wouldn't have liked what you saw. *I didn't like the man facing me in the mirror.* But I read the good word, prayed a lot, and found my way to forgiveness. Abby needed me, so I had no other choice."

"We always have a choice."

"You know what I mean. I needed to pull myself together for her."

Essie's heart softened. "You're right. Thank you for talking some sense into me. And for not judging me. It's hard to admit how I feel about Norma."

"I could never think badly of you."

"Never?"

The question hung in the air between them. She'd walked away from him, crushing his dreams. If anyone should withhold forgiveness from her, it was him.

"No, never." He let go of her hand and glanced over at the mountains before continuing. "Sure, I was hurt. Questioned a *lot*. But I never doubted that you have a good heart. I didn't know what your feelings toward me were. I struggled through my emotions, but never resented you as a person."

She held his gaze, unable to speak.

How could she have walked away from such a kindhearted man? She hadn't meant to, but she'd surely broken his heart and stomped on it.

At least she'd been given the chance to make things right.

But was that the *only* reason their lives had been thrust together?

CHAPTER 8

Noah ran his hands through his hair one last time so it didn't look so stiff from the gel. Then he straightened his tie and checked on Abby.

She was by the front door, and was struggling with the strap of her shoe because her holiday dress was so puffy.

"Let me get that." He squatted, fixing it almost instantly.

She beamed at him. "Thanks."

"You ready, kiddo?"

Abby grabbed her coat. "Is Essie coming to church with us?"

A warmth spread through him at the thought of how those two had taken to each other over the last few days. Essie had joined them for most meals, and had even insisted on cooking dinner the night before. The afternoon before that, she'd helped Abby with a psalm she was memorizing for school.

"Uncle Noah?" Abby waved her hand in front of his face, giggling. "Is she coming with us?"

Guilt pricked for not thinking of that himself. "She goes to her own church."

"But she doesn't have a car. Did you ask her?"

"No. She likely asked someone for a ride to her church. Scarlett, for example. She already knows where this place is."

"Maybe she didn't. Come on." Abby grabbed his arm and yanked him toward the door.

Noah laughed. "Let me get my jacket. There's two inches of snow on the grass."

"Hurry. She might need time to get ready."

He hadn't thought of that. If she hadn't gotten ready yet, she might not want to go. He zipped up his coat and grabbed a scarf.

Abby tugged on his arm. "Come *on*."

"Okay. Let's ask her." Worst that could happen was that they'd be late for the service if she needed time to get ready.

His niece pulled him all the way to the guesthouse and knocked on the door.

"Not so loud. She might be sleeping."

"Then she needs to get up." Abby banged with both fists.

Noah shook his head. Hopefully she wouldn't find all the knocking annoying.

A moment later, the door opened. Essie stood there in a simple cream-colored dress with half of her hair pulled back. She was gorgeous.

His heart sank. She was already planning on going to her own church. He should've known.

Abby stepped forward. "You wanna come to church with us? We're about to leave now."

Noah cleared his throat. "I think she's already going—"

"I'd love to." Essie smiled. "Just let me text Scarlett and let her know I'll be going with you two instead."

He gave his niece a knowing look.

She returned the same expression to him.

Noah chuckled.

Essie glanced up from her phone and gave them a questioning look.

"Inside joke," Abby said.

Five minutes later, Noah was starting the SUV. That too had been Adam's. Almost everything in Noah's life now had started out as his brother's.

He'd return it all in a heartbeat if it meant getting them back. But that would never happen.

"Turn on the Christmas music, Uncle Noah."

Essie turned back to Abby. "Great idea."

Noah found one of the stations that played it all month long, and *Silent Night* filled the car. As he pulled off the long driveway onto the road, Abby sang along. A moment later, Essie joined in.

Her voice took his breath away. She could sing a solo, and the entire congregation would give her a standing ovation. But he actually preferred being part of a private audience. Being close enough that he could reach over and hold her hand again.

It was tempting, but this was different than the other day when she'd been upset and had obviously been crying before he showed up. Plus, Abby was in the car. And it wasn't like he and Essie were dating again. She was still trying to get to Guatemala.

For five years.

But he'd waited this long, what was another time gap? If they were meant to be, then it wouldn't matter. They'd still have their entire lives to be together. Abby would be thirteen when Essie returned, and the girl she was adopting would be ten. They could be a proper family.

He was crazy for thinking such thoughts, but he couldn't help himself. Not with seeing Essie every day, and not when he'd never been able to find anyone who lived up to her.

"Aren't you going to sing?" Abby's voice broke through his thoughts.

The song had changed to *The First Noel*, and both Abby and Essie were belting out the lyrics. They sounded better than the choir over the speakers.

He joined in, his bass voice blending in perfectly with theirs.

It was like a dream come true, even if their time with Essie didn't last much past the holidays.

Noah would take what he could get.

CHAPTER 9

Essie sat on the pew, her heart full. The singing had really helped to heal her wounded heart—or at least begin the process. And it wasn't only singing with the congregation. It had started in the car with Abby and Noah.

Her conflicted feelings were completely gone. At first, she felt guilty about not going to her church but she really didn't want to face anyone after the mess of the mission trip. Everything was too raw, and she didn't feel like shedding more tears.

This was perfect. With Noah and Abby on either side of her now, she felt right at home. And it encouraged her heart to meet new people. There were actually a few familiar faces—people she'd met in various places around town. One from her old apartment building, another through work.

And now a teenager was sharing her testimony. It was such a powerful story about escaping abuse, recovering from addiction, and turning her life around by the power of God. And all at such a young age. It was enough to bring tears to her eyes. It helped comfort Essie. If that girl could get through all of that, God could surely fix Essie's problems.

Noah glanced over at her and smiled, his dimple showing. That only ever happened when he was truly happy.

A warmth flushed through her as she returned the gesture.

Thankfully, the congregation rose, and she didn't have to think about the rush of feelings coursing through her. But even so, that didn't change the fact that he was right next to her.

She prayed she'd be able to focus on the sermon. If he was too distracting, next week she would have to go to her church with Scarlett. Assuming, of course, that she didn't find a way to Guatemala by then.

The peppy Christmas carol was just the distraction she needed. Abby even took her hand and danced a little.

Once they sat and opened their Bibles—or apps on their phones—to read the word along with the preacher, Essie felt normal again.

Until she glanced over at Noah. She turned her head so quickly, she was fortunate she didn't give herself whiplash.

He was far too much of a distraction. It really made no sense why God had brought them back into each other's lives. She could've made it right with him without living on his property or coming to church with him.

She needed to focus more on getting to Guatemala. He'd already given her a paycheck as an advance for taking care of the horses, and she planned on putting most of that aside. It wasn't hard since she was eating most meals with him and Abby. And really enjoying it.

The next morning she would need to call Sarah and discuss updates on the upcoming fundraiser. She just needed a plane ticket and a ride to the orphanage. And a place to stay for her and Daniela—that had all been a farce cooked up by Norma to run off with the money.

Essie shoved those thoughts aside, but the prick of hurt and annoyance didn't leave. The situation was over and done with, so she needed to move on. Feelings included.

As if an answer from above, the sermon was about forgiveness, so Essie underlined every scripture to meditate on later.

Once the message was over, they sang a few more songs and sat through some announcements before the pastor dismissed them.

"What did you think?" Noah had a twinkle in his eye. He must've known that was exactly what she needed to hear.

Warmth crept into her cheeks. "It really spoke to me. I'm going to commit one or two of those scriptures to memory."

"That's a great idea. Maybe we could make it a competition."

"A competition?" She couldn't help smiling at the idea.

"Just a friendly one, of course."

"Sounds like fun."

Abby tugged on Noah's sleeve. "I'm going to go say hi to my friends."

"Okay."

Essie watched Abby run off to a group of girls about the same age. "She doesn't have a class she could go to during the sermon?"

Noah's expression turned wistful. "She could, but she always wants to stay by me. I think she's worried that something might happen to me."

"I can't imagine what it must be like to go through losing her parents at such a young age."

"Me neither, but I'm glad I can be here for her, and she's still hearing the word."

Essie started to say something, but a lady in her thirties introduced herself as Audrey, giving Essie a warm hug.

"You have such a beautiful family." She glanced over at Noah then to Abby with her friends.

Essie's face burned. "We're not—"

"Are you coming to the Christmas party this coming Friday evening? It's going to be so much fun. And you can stay as late as you want since the next morning is Saturday, assuming of course you don't have other plans. Several of the teens are even offering babysitting—anything you pay will be donated toward their summer camp."

Essie turned to Noah, unsure what to say.

He smiled widely and put his arm around her. "We haven't talked about it yet, but it sounds like it would be great fun."

"Oh, it will." Audrey beamed. "I'm on the planning committee, and I don't want to give away any surprises, but it's going to be the event of the year. Invite your friends and family." Someone tapped her shoulder and Audrey turned back to Essie. "It was so nice meeting you. Hope to see you next weekend."

Before Essie could respond, the other woman was already deep in her next conversation.

Noah chuckled.

That reminded Essie that his arm was still around her. And she really liked it. His presence and touch were both comforting and protective at the same time. She hadn't realized how much she needed someone to care for her. And he'd stepped in to fill that role in so many ways since her move had been canceled.

Abby ran over and tugged on Noah. "Can I go to Lily's house for the afternoon?"

Noah stepped away from Essie. "I don't know. You have that math test to study for."

"Please, Uncle Noah." Abby pressed her palms together. "I promise I'll study tonight. Plus I got ninety percent on the quiz last week."

"I don't know. You still have your chores too."

"I'll get it all done. I promise! And Lily's mom said she'd drop me off. You won't even have to drive."

Noah glanced at Essie. "What are your plans for the afternoon?"

"Mine?" She tried to cover her surprise. "Nothing other than laundry."

"Will you join me for lunch? I was thinking about trying that new restaurant by the lake."

Essie hesitated. She would have to watch what she spent because she wanted to put as much into her Guatemala fund as possible. "Okay."

"Great." Noah smiled and turned to Abby. "Let me talk with Lily's mom real quick, but I'm sure it's a go."

Abby squealed and threw her arms around him. "Thank you!"

Essie couldn't help smiling. Noah was such a good uncle-turned-dad, and seeing them interact made her heart soar. He was the same kindhearted person he'd always been.

Noah put his hand on her shoulder. "I'll be right back."

She nodded and sat back down as she watched the two of them speak with another family. Her feelings when he was around were overwhelming. She'd seen many other father-daughter pairs, but none had anywhere near the same effect on her.

And she kind of liked it.

CHAPTER 10

Noah finished his last bite of his steak and wiped his mouth. He was full in every way possible—not just his belly, but his spirit and his heart as well.

Essie was distracted eating her pasta dish—it had taken some serious convincing to get her to order more than a salad and let him pay for her meal. He took advantage of the moment to soak in her beauty. Every move she made was full of grace, and he swore she had managed to become even more gorgeous in the time since she'd walked back into his life.

The problem was, the longer she stayed, the harder the idea of letting go again became. This wasn't just catching up with someone from his past.

He was falling in love again—if he'd ever fallen out. The fact that nobody else lived up to her made him think he'd been living in denial. It wasn't like the others had been bad people. They had each been beautiful and lovable in their own right.

The problem had been that they weren't Essie.

Now that she was back in his life, he didn't know what he would do when she left. He was digging his own heart's grave by paying her to take care of the horses. With each new check he would give her, she'd be that much closer to moving to another country.

And waiting five years for her return was sounding less and less doable with every passing moment.

Could he move with her? What about Abby and the ten-acre property? It wouldn't be fair to uproot her from not only the only home she knew, but also the culture. A quick mission trip was one thing, but a five-year move was something else altogether.

Especially within a year of the plane crash.

He had to think about her needs above his own. She was his daughter now.

Essie cleared her throat, pulling him from his thoughts. She smiled at him.

Noah beamed. He had to look ridiculous grinning like a fool, but he didn't care. Not when he was with her.

"Thanks again for lunch." She dabbed her mouth with her napkin.

"It was my pleasure. Thank you for joining me."

"Honestly, I'd have been fine with a salad."

"Don't mention it." He paid for the meal and they climbed back into Adam's SUV.

Would he ever think of anything as his? It wasn't like his brother was coming back to claim any of it.

The thought made his heart hurt.

On the way to the house, they passed the cemetery.

He turned to Essie. "Mind if we stop? I'd like to visit my family."

Her expression fell. "Of course. I'm so sorry you can only visit them here."

"At least I can visit them. Some of the passengers were never found."

Essie gasped.

"Sorry. Was that too grim?"

"No, not at all. I just feel so bad for all the families. That would add to the grief in ways I can't imagine."

He cleared his throat and turned on his blinker.

The walk to his family's grave markers was a sobering one. The stones went on far into the distance.

Leaving this earth was something nobody could escape. He didn't want to think about what it must be like for the people who had no hope after death.

Essie slid her hand into his.

The gesture surprised him and he turned to her.

She gave him a sad smile. "We haven't reached them yet, and you already have a tear."

"Do I?" He wiped his eye, a single tear trailing onto the back of his hand. "I didn't even realize."

Essie squeezed his hand, and he felt stronger.

He stopped at the familiar graves grouped together. The last flowers he and Abby had brought were dried and wilted, covered in snow. Someone else had brought a bouquet more recently, and some of the flowers still looked alive.

Essie stepped closer and wrapped her arm around his waist. "I'm so sorry for your loss. I can't believe they're gone. Your parents were the sweetest people, and Adam was always so kind. He had a great sense of humor."

"He did." Noah smiled as he recalled a prank his brother had pulled, which left Noah sticky and covered in feathers.

"What was Cora like?"

"She was perfect for him. Smart as a whip like Abby. Sweet too. You'd have really liked her."

"I'm sure I would have."

Noah sighed and leaned his head against Essie's. Her presence gave him strength. This was the first time he'd been here without falling apart inside. He almost always kept himself together on the outside for Abby's sake—not that they hadn't shared tears here.

What would his parents think of him being here with Essie? His mom had always thought he should've fought harder for her. But what was he supposed to have done? Flown out to Romania and declared his love?

Now it was Guatemala.

If Noah asked for her hand in marriage again, he would only hold her back. He didn't mind the idea of traveling, but the thought of not returning home for years at a time made his throat dry.

But if he was with Essie, would it have been so bad? If they were together, then home would be wherever she was.

He studied each inscription, thinking about each of the people he'd lost. What would they say to him if they were still here?

His parents and brother had all liked Essie, so they might encourage him to go after his dream. Or his brother and Cora might prefer he stay at the house and focus on Abby.

That would be the responsible thing to do.

CHAPTER 11

❄

Essie sipped the hot cocoa and watched the lights blinking on the Christmas tree. An instrumental version of *O Holy Night* played in the background as the crackling fire warmed her from behind.

Next to her, Noah set his mug down. "Thanks for going to the cemetery with me. I know it isn't a fun place to visit, especially this time of year."

"I'm glad I could be there for you. It can't be easy with this being your first Christmas season without them."

He gave her an appreciative smile. "No, but it does help to have you here. Abby has really taken to you."

"I really like her too." She hesitated before continuing.

"What is it?" Noah rested his hand on her back and tilted his head.

She looked back at the tree before turning to him again. "I'm glad you asked me to stay in your guesthouse. I know we've both had disappointing years—yours much worse than mine— but it's been good to reconnect. I didn't realize how much I needed to apologize for how I treated you."

He rubbed circles on her back. "I forgave you long ago, Es."

Her heart skipped a beat at the use of the nickname. It had been something only he had ever called her. Essie was already a shortened version of her given name Esther, after her grandmother and also the character from the Bible.

"Have you forgiven yourself?" Noah asked.

"What?"

"It seems to me like you're carrying around a lot of guilt over how we parted. Maybe I'm wrong."

She frowned, unable to deny it. "I do feel bad. It wasn't right to run off like that. At the very least, you deserved an explanation."

He took both her hands in his. "It wasn't that hard to figure out. I scared you off, and you threw yourself into the work you love."

Her heart threatened to explode out of her chest and her hands shook in his. "Yes, but I also loved you."

Noah jolted slightly. Because she used love in the past tense? Or for some other reason?

She blinked back tears. "The way I treated you was really the lowest thing I've ever done. You didn't deserve it, and acting like that wasn't me. Except it was. I have to take responsibility for my actions."

He held her gaze, his chocolate eyes melting her. "It's all in the past. Let's focus on the future. Or at least the now."

Pop!

She jumped, the fire behind them sounding like a weapon, and took a deep breath. "What is the future?"

He cupped her chin and leaned close enough that she could smell the mint from the candy canes in their cocoa on his breath. "It's anything we want it to be."

Her breath hitched, her pulse thrummed in her ears.

What *did* she want with him? Could they have a future

together? It didn't seem possible, which was why she'd run away all those years before, but maybe if they talked about it together they could figure out something that would work for both of them.

Then she wouldn't have to choose between him and the mission field. Maybe he would want to join her. Or perhaps she could travel less to be with him. She was crazy if she didn't think their own town was a mission field with so many churches closing their doors in recent months.

Could this be the field she was meant to focus on instead? Was that why she still felt so drawn to this wonderful and godly man who was looking at her like he wanted to kiss her? She pushed those thoughts aside. Why would she be called to stay locally when her family was all over the world? It made no sense.

"What do you want the future to be?" Noah asked, his breath tickling her cheek.

Essie's heart shouted to tell him how she felt. But her tongue wouldn't cooperate.

"Do you want me in your life?" He inched closer.

Unable to speak, she nodded.

Noah pressed his lips on her mouth and his hands tightened around hers.

Her heart pounded like a jackhammer, yet it also soared beyond the ceiling. This was even better than any of the other kisses they'd shared when they were younger. She leaned in closer, savoring the moment.

Almost as soon as it started, it was over. He pulled away, a dazed look in his eyes. "That was worth waiting all that time for."

So many things raced through her mind, she didn't know which to speak.

Noah saved her from deciding by pulling her close. His heart thump-thumped in her ear and she breathed in the rugged scent of his cologne.

Knock, knock!

He rose, helping her up. "Sounds like Abby's back."

"Better get the door." At least her voice was still working.

As she listened to Noah greeting his niece and her friend's mom, Essie sat back down. In her mind, she relived the kiss, her pulse racing as if his lips were once again on hers.

She finished her cocoa, trying to bring herself back to the current moment.

Abby's footsteps tapped on the hardwood as she skipped over. Essie gave her a hug. "Did you have fun?"

"Lily got a trampoline as an early Christmas present! We bounced until we couldn't feel our legs anymore."

"In the snow?"

"Her dad swept off the snow and we both wore three pairs of socks and our winter coats." Abby beamed. "It was the *best*."

Essie laughed. "I'll have to take your word for it."

"I need to add a trampoline to my Christmas list. Think Uncle Noah will buy one?"

"I'm not sure. It seems like it would be hard to get one this time of year."

"Lily got one."

"That's true."

The front door closed, and Noah made his way over. "What's this I hear about a trampoline for Christmas?"

"Please." Abby smiled widely and batted her lashes.

Noah laughed. "You sure make it hard to say no to."

Abby threw her arms around him.

"I didn't say yes. You have a test to study for and chores."

"On it!" She bounded down the hall.

Noah shook his head with a grin.

"You're a really good uncle."

"I sure hope so. The last thing I want to do is let her down."

"That won't happen."

He cupped her chin and gazed into her eyes. "That kiss was amazing. I hope there'll be more of that."

"So do I." She couldn't keep the smile off her face.

CHAPTER 12

Noah headed for the stables—something that had become part of his morning routine. His favorite part, if he was being honest with himself.

If Essie was on schedule, she should just be finishing up with the horses. Then they could go on a little walk since the weather wasn't too bad. It was actually a little sunny, making the vapors from his breath all the more visible this morning.

It might be their last morning walk for a while since today was Abby's last day of school before the holiday, and starting tomorrow he'd have to keep her entertained all day. He'd managed it all summer—some vacationing had helped—but for some reason her Christmas break made him nervous. He couldn't put his finger on it, but it was probably because Adam and Cora had laid the foundation with so many holiday traditions. Noah was sure to mess something up.

But today was just another day. Another day with Essie at the guesthouse, taking care of the horses and joining them for meals.

His heart soared at the thought. It was hard to imagine he'd been so blessed. He'd basically given up on love—the romantic kind. After realizing there would be no filling the Essie-sized hole in his life, he'd thrown himself into work. Now into his niece.

And somehow God had seen fit to bring Essie back into his life. They'd even been growing closer and closer. He hadn't kissed her again even though he hadn't stopped thinking about their kiss on Sunday in front of the fireplace. The last thing he wanted to do was to push anything too quickly or come across as ungrateful for the blessing.

They'd grown closer over the past few days, opening up about their respective dreams and heartaches and even reminiscing some over their past memories.

Noah hoped and prayed their futures would continue to intersect. Essie was still determined to get to Guatemala, though lately she spoke less of the mission field and more of retrieving the little girl. She was so grateful the adoption had gone through—thank God that she had been working with someone else on that other than the lady who had run off with everyone's mission money.

One fact that Noah hadn't been able to bring up was that he could easily pay for her plane ticket down and back. He'd had a growing prick of guilt over that with each passing day, but he couldn't bring himself to voice it.

What if she took him up on it and flew down for the next five years? It would crush him. He wanted her in his life as long as possible, selfish as that was. But it wasn't like he was trying to prevent her trip. He'd given her a quiet place to stay and was paying her to take care of the horses—something he'd been doing himself and could continue doing with no problem.

Sighing, he opened the stable door and stepped in. The thought of offering her a plane ticket was inching away from the back of his mind and closer to his mouth.

Essie set down a bag of feed and turned to him, smiling. She brushed her ponytail behind her shoulder and dusted off her hands. "Good morning."

All of his worries melted away. "'Morning, sunshine."

She came over and wrapped her arms around him.

He held her close, never wanting to let go. Embracing her was like hanging onto a piece of Heaven.

"Need any help?" he asked.

Essie gave him a playful shove. "You ask after I finish everything."

Noah chuckled. "I can't help my timing. With it being Abby's last day of school until the new year, I had a bunch of papers to sign. I'm not even fully sure what I agreed to. Got tired of reading all the fine print."

"I can understand that, and I'm sure she appreciates it." She squeezed his hand. "You want to go for a walk?"

"I'd love nothing more." Except to propose. He shoved that thought so far it probably landed in Europe somewhere. There was no way he was going to do that anytime soon. Or maybe even ever. He'd have to be fully assured she wouldn't turn him down again.

Her smile lit up the entire stable. "Great. Let me just grab a water bottle from the guesthouse. I'm parched. You want one?"

"Sure. Thanks." He held the door for her and waited outside while she hurried in.

It took her a while, and he started to worry that something was wrong.

He cracked open the door. "Everything okay?"

"I'm almost done," she called.

"Just checking." He stepped back outside and took in the skyline. The mountains beyond the trees weren't just snow-capped, they were fully white. It was a breathtaking sight with the blue sky behind them. He'd adjusted to the gray clouds.

The door creaked open—he'd have to fix that for her—and she appeared with two water bottles in hand, now wearing clean clothes. Not that she'd looked bad in the dusty ones. She could never look less than perfect.

Essie handed him a bottle. "Here you go."

"Thanks."

"I should be thanking you. You bought them."

"Doesn't matter. They're yours now. Should we take our typical path?"

She lifted a brow. "Is there another one?"

"There are plenty. Some I haven't explored yet."

Her eyes lit up. "That sounds like fun."

"Maybe when we don't have to worry about ice."

"Oh." Her expression fell but then brightened. "The regular path, it is."

He slid his fingers through hers.

She squeezed his hand and they walked in silence for a few minutes before she spoke. "So, what are your plans for Christmas?"

The question threw him for a moment. "Just opening presents with Abby that morning. We already had the family dinner."

"Sounds nice and relaxing." Her tone indicated an unasked question.

Then it struck him. She had nowhere to go. Her family was spread across the globe and she'd been expecting to be in Guatemala with her adopted daughter.

"You're more than welcome to join us," he said quickly. "I can't guarantee it'll be exciting though."

She looked away. "I don't want to intrude."

He stopped and looked at her. "You're never in the way. Not with me. Please get that idea out of your mind."

Her expression softened. "Are you sure? I already take up so much of your time."

The words stung, but he tried to hide it. "Do you really feel that way?"

"I don't feel like I really belong anywhere."

"You belong here."

She didn't look like she believed him.

"You do. Both Abby and I really like having you here." His voice came out gruffer than he'd meant. He took her hand again, and they walked toward the path in the forest. Neither said a word.

Noah took in the woodsy aromas—mostly the sweet smell of decaying leaves but with other earthy tones. It helped calm his nerves.

He sent up a silent prayer before stopping at a brook that was now mostly ice and turned to Essie. "Do you really feel that way?"

"That I don't belong?"

Noah nodded.

She frowned.

"Why?" he asked.

"I shouldn't even be here. My family isn't even on this continent. I'm not accomplishing anything with my time. Every day that I'm here Daniela has to spend in an orphanage."

"And whose doing is that?"

Her eyebrows drew together. "What do you mean?"

"None of that is your fault. A deceitful woman prevented your trip from happening. Your family chose against gathering together for Christmas. I for one am glad you're here. So's Abby."

Her gaze fell. "I'm sorry. I didn't mean to sound ungrateful. Your family isn't even able to celebrate with you, and here I am—"

"I didn't say any of that to shame you. My only point is that you *do* belong. I'm not sure why God put you here at this time, but I'm not about to question a good thing."

She glanced back at him. "You really mean that?"

"Your return is the best thing that's happened all year. I

never thought I'd see you again, and yet here we are." He squeezed her hand.

Tears shone in her eyes.

His heart shattered. "Don't be sad on my account." He drew a deep breath and tried to figure out how to fix the situation. "I just want to focus on what's good. You're here with me, and we're in the middle of this amazing display of creation. Can we just enjoy the moment and not worry about the future?"

Her mouth curved up slightly. "I'll try. I do like being with you."

Noah pulled her close and as he started to pull away, a thought struck him. "Will you come with me to the church Christmas party on Friday night?"

"I'd love to, but …" Her voice trailed off.

"But what?"

She frowned. "I don't have anything nearly nice enough to wear. That dress I wore to your family dinner was Scarlett's and the one I wore to church isn't festive."

He stood taller. "I can fix that."

"You can?"

"Yes. I'll drop you off at the mall on my way to pick up Abby from school. You can pick up whatever you want."

"I don't have much money. It all—"

"You can take my credit card. Like I said, get whatever you want. Don't stop with a party dress. I've noticed you don't have many winter clothes. Get some of those too."

Her mouth gaped and tears shone in her eyes. "You can't mean that."

"Of course I do. I know you sold everything and only saved what you'd need in a tropical climate. I've been given plenty. Allow me to share some of that with you."

A single tear trailed down her face. "I don't know what to say."

"Say yes." He wiped the tear away and kissed her cheek. "Nothing would make me happier."

"Yes."

Warmth spread through him and he kissed the top of her head.

CHAPTER 13

Essie stared at her reflection in disbelief. It was hard to accept that the elegant woman staring back at her was actually her. The ruby-red dress brought out the best in her coloring, and with her hair curled like this, the way it framed her face made her look like a completely different person. Especially with the extra makeup. She usually wore little more than mascara and lip gloss, but thanks to the samples she'd received at the mall, she'd been able to do a full makeover with the help of a video online.

Knock, knock.

Her heart nearly exploded.

Noah was here.

What would he think of how she looked? Would he think she was overdone and ridiculous? Or would he still think she was pretty?

Maybe she'd gone too far with the makeup. It was silly. Prideful.

Knock, knock!

"Hold on!"

Her breathing grew labored as she stared at her reflection. She looked like royalty.

As a child of God the King, she was a princess.

But that wasn't how she looked. It was more like one of the princesses always displayed on the magazines.

It wasn't her.

She should wash off all the makeup. People would talk about her behind her back.

Knock, knock.

There was no time, and she was being rude making Noah wait outside in the cold.

She glanced in the mirror at the simple cross necklace she wore, hoping that would help her decide what the best option was.

"Are you okay in there?" Noah called from the other side of the door.

"Yes!" Frowning, she looked at her jarring reflection. She could never get used to all of the makeup.

But she did come to a decision—if Noah liked it, she would keep it. If he didn't, she would apologize and wash it all off.

Pulse pounding, she hurried to the door, her ankle nearly rolling in the new high-heeled pumps. Her mouth went dry as she opened the door. She prepared herself for Noah's look of horror.

She stood tall and smiled, trying to cover her worry as much as the makeup covered her face.

Noah stood there, more handsome than ever in a suit and tie that made him appear even taller and broader than normal. He was the textbook definition of male perfection.

His eyes widened as he stared at her face, his mouth gaped slightly.

Her heart sunk.

"You're beyond gorgeous." He slid a red and white corsage onto her wrist that matched her dress perfectly.

She blinked a few times. "You really think so?"

He nodded slowly. "Give me a moment to pick up my jaw off the floor so I can speak a coherent sentence."

Relief washed through her, relaxing her. "You don't think I'm overdone?"

"Not at all." He stepped closer and brushed his fingertips along her jawline, holding her gaze. "The makeup brings out your best features."

What a relief.

He cleared his throat and stood taller. "Are you ready?"

She grabbed her new coat and turned off the lights. "I am. Will Abby be joining us?"

Noah looped his arm through hers. "I dropped her off at a friend's from school. She's going to spend the night so we don't have to worry about what time we need to leave. They're having a kiddy party that she was begging me to attend, and I certainly wasn't going to complain about spending the evening with just you."

"So this is a date?" The words flew from her mouth before she had a chance to filter them.

"If you'd like it to be." The hope in his eyes was undeniable.

She swallowed. "I would."

He beamed. "Before you walked back into my life, I never thought this Christmas could have any real joy. But now it does."

"I feel the same way."

The ride to the church building went by in a blur of festive music and Noah holding her hand at every stoplight. Everything was moving so fast, but she didn't want to put an end to any of it. It was a whirlwind of joy and hope.

Everything the holiday was supposed to be.

When they arrived at the party, everything was in full swing. The fellowship hall was decorated with wreaths and tinsel, and had a band playing festive music. At the other end of the room tables were filled with food. Many were already eating and others were playing games.

Noah turned to her. "What would you like to do first?"

"I'd love to try some of the food."

As they stood in line, several ladies complimented Essie's dress. And again, some people assumed she and Noah were married. Obviously, they were people who didn't know him. Several of his friends introduced themselves, seeming pleased that he wasn't there alone.

Everything on her plate was so delicious she was tempted to go back for seconds, but she wanted to make sure everyone had a chance to get what they wanted.

They joined a game of Christmas Pictionary, and she laughed so hard she almost cried when Noah drew what looked like the three wise men but was really Mary and Joseph traveling on the donkey to Bethlehem. Their team obviously lost that round.

After that, they decorated cookies for a contest. This time it was Noah's turn to laugh at her. She had many talents, but adding frosting to desserts was not one of them.

They both shone at the game of guessing the Christmas carol. After winning the round, they continued making their way through the room, playing more games than Essie had in a long time, probably since she was a kid.

As they came to the last activity, her heart sped up. It was a photo station.

She and Noah hadn't had a picture together since they'd reconnected. Even though it probably shouldn't seem like a big deal, it felt monumental.

Like it was shoving them back into official couple status. Not that the hand holding and him kissing her hadn't.

This made it feel like there was no turning back.

Proof of them being a couple.

He turned to her with a twinkle in his eyes. "You want to?"

Essie forced a smile. "Yes, of course."

Noah put his arm around her and led her to the backdrop of a snowy scene with a bright star above a manger.

The camerawoman directed their pose, having them hold each other's hands and lean in close while smiling. Essie focused on how great the evening had been rather than her concern for what the photo represented.

Maybe Noah would see it as nothing more than a picture.

Doubtful.

She pushed her worries aside as they made their way back to the cookie table to see who had won the contest. At least she knew it wouldn't be her.

Except they'd awarded her with Most Creative.

Most Awful was more like it, but she laughed and took her certificate, relaxing again.

Noah slid his hand around hers, and she felt even more at ease. She was probably making a bigger deal about the picture than necessary. People took pictures together all the time. What was the harm in it? It was a way to remember the evening, no matter how things turned out between them. If they went their separate ways, then she would always smile when she looked at the photo.

The hall was beginning to thin out but they played another round of Christmas Carol Bingo before heading out. The photographer handed them each a copy of their picture in a red-and-green paper frame.

Noah's expression lit up as he looked it over. Then he kissed the top of her head. "I think this is the best picture of us we've ever taken."

"Not that it's hard to beat the awkward teen and early adult years."

"You were never awkward." He took her coat off the rack and helped her put it on.

"Are you kidding?" She laughed before shuddering at the

thought. "My neck and feet had growth spurts before the rest of me. Then there was that awful bout with my skin."

"I never saw you as anything other than beautiful. Ever." He pulled on his jacket and snickered. "Me, on the other hand—if you look up awkward in the dictionary, you'll see my lanky, frizzy-haired Sophomore picture."

Essie shook her head. "You weren't that bad."

"So you admit I was kind of gawky?"

"I already said we both were. That's just part of life."

He laughed and held open the car door for her. "That's true."

They shared funny stories from their high school and college years until they reached the guesthouse.

Noah took her hands in his again and looked at her with a mixture of elation and fatigue. "Tonight was really fun. I hope we can have more dates like this one."

She leaned against him and rested her head against his shoulder. "So do I."

He tilted her chin up toward him, and she got lost in his eyes.

Noah leaned in and brushed his lips across hers. "I love you, Es. I really do."

Essie's heart plummeted.

He didn't seem to notice her reaction, keeping his gaze locked on her eyes. "You don't have to respond. I just wanted you to know."

With that, he strolled toward his house.

She stared, hardly able to breathe.

CHAPTER 14

❄

Essie woke, gasping for air in the tangle of blankets. She'd had yet another distressing dream—they'd plagued her all night.

It was just after seven. She may as well get up and start the day.

She still couldn't believe Noah had said those three words.

I love you.

He hadn't even noticed her shock.

She picked up the picture from the night before on the headboard. They looked like the perfect couple.

A photo of Daniela caught her eye. She picked that up and compared the two images.

Her adopted daughter had a genuine smile, though not as wide as the ones Essie and Noah wore in their picture from the night before. Daniela's clothes had dirt stains and a few holes. She also didn't wear shoes, but Essie kept telling herself that was by choice because of the heat. But was it?

Guilt stung as Essie's gaze moved to the picture of her and Noah in the expensive clothes after eating what had to look like a feast in the little girl's eyes.

How could she live in the lap of luxury while her daughter was wasting away in a third-world orphanage? Especially when she should've already been there to pick her up. Granted the little home she was going to bring Daniela back to in Guatemala was little more than a shack, but at least she would have a mom. Not just caregivers.

Although from what she'd heard, the women who worked in the orphanage really did care about the children and were said to treat them well, it wasn't the same as having a home. A mom.

Essie sat up straight, trying not to look at the photo of her and Noah, but as she put them back his smile caught her attention. She stopped and got lost in his eyes, a warmth spreading throughout her body, starting at her chest. His declaration of love the night before ran through her mind, followed by images from their walks and the two kisses he'd given her. He was a kind and godly man who obviously loved her, not to mention also a great dad to Abby. She couldn't deny her feelings for him.

But now she was facing the same dilemma she'd faced those years earlier. They lived in two different worlds with completely different dreams and goals. And those worlds couldn't be any more different.

She compared the two photos again. As much as she loved her time with Noah, it was selfish. There was no way to help Daniela and others like her when she was living like this. She couldn't be like the rest of her family if she wasn't also living in a different part of the world helping the poor and spreading the good news.

A lump formed in her throat. She knew what she needed to do.

It seemed like a cruel joke to have to make this decision twice, and with the same person. The last thing she wanted to do was hurt Noah again. But there was no getting around it—she wouldn't give up her dream of living as a missionary to spread the word and take care of the poor.

Hurting him was unavoidable, and she had nobody to blame but herself. She'd allowed herself to get wrapped up in feelings instead of staying on course. It had probably been a bad idea to call him and ask to stay here in the guesthouse. A temptation.

Except that she'd prayed about it. The answer had been clear. But why?

Now she would have to break his heart again. But at least she'd matured, grown from the young woman who'd simply run away.

He would understand. He had to. If he really loved her like he said, he would find a way to accept the fact that they couldn't realistically be together.

She would shower and get dressed, then have the hard discussion with him. That would give her time to pray for the right words. She would need to explain her reasons and ask for his forgiveness.

Then she could move on. And that would have to be literally. She couldn't face him after breaking the news to him. He would be crushed, especially after how much fun they'd had the night before.

Tears stung her eyes at the thought of walking away from what they'd built over the short time she'd been staying there. But it was the right thing to do. It would be even harder if she stayed until she had the funds to leave for Guatemala.

It was now or never.

Her mind swirled as she got ready. She had to lean against the wall for support a few times as her breath grew short and it became hard to breathe.

She decided to head to the stables to work before going to the house to talk with Noah. It was the right thing to do, since she'd agreed to do that much for him. First, she fell to her knees and begged God for the right words and for Noah's heart to be understanding, that he would be prepared before she broke the news.

As Essie headed for the stables, her breathing became labored. She kept imagining the disappointment on his face, and it got worse every time she saw it in her mind.

Taking care of the horses didn't help. She realized she would miss them too. Tears stung and her voice cracked as she spoke to them.

If she was falling apart with the animals, how much harder would this be to talk to Noah?

It would be next to impossible. She would completely lose it, especially when he tried to talk her out of it. What then? Would she give in to him and decide to stay in the states? Give up her dream of mission work?

Her parents would be so disappointed in her. They'd raised her to love and cherish their life's work. It had always been her desire to follow in their footsteps.

She just needed to get to Guatemala to get her daughter. Surely she could find mission work once there. In fact, the options would be so abundant she would probably have a hard time choosing where to serve.

Now it was only a matter of getting down there. She'd managed to save most of what Noah had paid her, only needing to buy a few things here and there. But the only reason she'd been able to do that was because she'd eaten his food and used his card to buy clothes.

Guilt stung. Maybe she should leave the money he'd given her and find another way to Guatemala. Then she wouldn't feel like she owed him.

Not that giving back the money would make up for walking away again.

But at least she would handle it better this time. She wouldn't leave without an explanation.

She would tell him exactly what she was thinking. He would understand. He wouldn't be happy, but they would part on good terms. He wouldn't have any lingering questions. He could move on.

The thought sucked the air right out of her lungs. She didn't want to imagine him looking at anyone else the way he looked at her. However, that was the way it had to be.

Wiping tears from her eyes, she said goodbye to the horses and hurried back to the guesthouse. She needed to wash her face before knocking on the door at the main house.

If she could handle facing him.

It would be easier to leave a note instead. Then he would have his answers and she could walk away without him tugging on her heartstrings.

It would already be hard enough. Maybe that was the right answer.

Once in the guesthouse, she dropped to her knees again to plead for answers.

CHAPTER 15

Noah could barely feel the snow-dusted ground beneath his feet as he made his way to the guesthouse. He hadn't slept much the night before, his mind on his date with Essie at the Christmas party.

It had been a dream come true. They had been like a real couple again, and she seemed happy to be with him.

They really had a chance. His heart soared high above the snow clouds that were threatening to release a downpour.

More than anything, he wanted to become a family with Essie. The two of them plus their adopted daughters. It would be perfect. Adam had left him so much money, they could adopt a whole quiver of children if that was what Essie wanted. Or they could have their own, but with so many children in need, he loved the idea of adopting even more.

Noah stopped in front of the guesthouse door and drew in a deep breath. He wanted to pull Essie into his arms the moment she appeared. Tell her how much he loved her and never wanted to let go.

It was a Christmas miracle. Just a few weeks ago, he'd thought he would never see her again. In fact, she hardly crossed his mind these days. After she'd first left, he thought almost exclusively of her no matter what he was doing. But now, she was living in the guesthouse. They'd had numerous heart-to-heart talks, he'd kissed her twice, and they had gone on as many dates.

This was both the worst year of his life and the best. He'd lost three of the people he'd loved the most, but then the other one walked back into it. Not that he could compare the losses to the gain, but her return was a monumental blessing—a bright light shining in a dark expanse.

He knocked and waited. Maybe she didn't hear. He knocked louder.

Still nothing.

Noah knocked again, this time calling her name.

After no response, he pressed his ear to the door. Didn't hear the shower running. No other noises. If he didn't know better, he'd think she wasn't there at all.

Maybe she'd gone to take care of the horses.

He knocked a final time before heading to the stable.

No Essie.

His heart sank. Something couldn't be wrong, could it?

Noah jogged back to the guesthouse and pounded on the door, yelling her name.

After getting the same response as before, he jiggled the knob expecting it to be locked.

It twisted open.

His stomach knotted. "Essie?"

The little building had an empty feel to it. It was hard to explain, but he couldn't shake it.

He stepped inside. The bed was made and all of her things were gone.

No, not everything. The clothes she'd bought with his credit card were folded on the table with the receipt on top and an envelope was on the nightstand on the other side of the bed.

Noah's pulse drummed in his ears as he darted over and picked up the folded paper first.

A note in her handwriting—he would always recognize her penmanship. It was burned into his memory.

The paper shook in his hand. He fell onto the bed and had to set the paper onto the pillow in order to read the words. But he didn't need to read what she'd written.

His heart already knew.

She had left him. Again.

First when he proposed, and now after saying that he loved her. He never should have told her how he felt. He should've known she was jumpy about anything even remotely resembling commitment.

Instead of thinking, he'd bared his heart on his sleeve.

And now she was gone.

Noah bolted to his feet and raced through the guesthouse in hopes that she hadn't left yet. That he could change her mind. Or at least try.

He needed to do that much.

After checking every room twice, he leaned against the kitchen counter. Rubbed his temples. Sent up desperate prayers.

Essie couldn't have gone far. Not without a car. And the only place she would head to would be Guatemala. And there was no way she could get there even with the money he'd paid her.

He whipped out his phone and called her. He should've done that the moment he realized she'd left.

Straight to voicemail. It was an automated message. He didn't even get to hear a recording of her voice.

He drew a shaky breath as he thought about what to say. If anything. She might not even listen to it. But there was always the chance she would, and he needed to say something.

Beep.

"Essie, please don't do this. We need to talk. We can make things work. There's a compromise, and we can find it. It doesn't have to be black or white. Our answer is somewhere in the shades of gray." He hesitated, almost saying that he loved her, but then ended the call. If him saying that the night before had scared her off, repeating it on the message would only make things worse.

Noah tried her number one more time.

Voicemail again.

He brushed hair from his eyes and tried to think straight. There had to be something he could do. Staying in the guesthouse wasn't accomplishing anything other than Essie getting farther away from him.

Had she called someone from her church to pick her up? Someone who would be able to offer her a place to stay? Or even someone who had the means to get her on a plane to Guatemala?

There was only one way to find out. He found Scarlett's number and called her.

"Hey cousin," she answered. "Merry almost-Christmas."

His insides twisted at the thought of the holiday without Essie. He cleared his throat. "You too. Hey, I have a quick question."

"Perfect. Quick is all I have time for. Connor is bouncing off the walls and I need to get him to the park."

"You haven't talked to Essie, have you?"

"Not in the last few days."

Noah raked his fingers through his hair. "Who is she close to at your church? Someone she might call if she needed something?"

"I'm not entirely sure. We've never been very close, what with her in the singles ministry and me in the marrieds."

"Why did you take her in? Bring her to the family gathering?"

"She had nowhere to go, and I was the last one in the church building. Taking her in was the right thing to do."

Noah drew a deep breath, trying not to let his frustration get the better of him. "You can't think of *anyone* she's friends with? Nobody?"

"I could ask the pastor's wife. I'm sure Sarah would know."

"Would you call her for me, and let me know what she says?"

"Yes. Is everything okay? She isn't in trouble, is she?"

"I don't think so." Noah paced, frustration building. "I mean, no. Essie's fine. I just can't reach her, and I really need to."

"Okay. I'll make a few calls and see what I can find out. Then I'll call you right back."

"I appreciate it. Thanks, Scarlett." Noah ended the call.

He hurried outside.

Noticed fresh footprints in the frosty grass that he hadn't seen before.

Essie had walked to the driveway. She was heading to the road on foot.

Maybe he could catch up to her if he hurried.

CHAPTER 16

Essie readjusted her backpack before picking her two suitcases up again. Walking to the nearest bus stop with all her luggage had been a crazy idea. Especially with the icy patches. Or at the very least, it would've been easier in warmer weather.

But she could do it. She needed to be on a bus before Noah realized she had left. He would understand. Maybe not right away, but eventually. It was better this way. Easier, anyway. For her.

A prick of guilt stung. She should've stuck with her original plan and spoken with him in person.

No. The note was perfectly acceptable. She'd explained everything exactly as she'd wanted. Writing it out had given her the time to think everything through. If she'd have said it spontaneously, no doubt she'd have stumbled over her words and forgotten important points. But now he would have all of her thoughts and he could read them over as many times as necessary.

She'd handled it the right way. Better than before. Everything would be good to go for her trip to Guatemala. No more reasons for it to be postponed. She'd closed everything up now.

Gravel crunched behind her.

Breath hitched, she spun around.

The only sound was a bird singing in the woods. Strange that it wouldn't have gone south already. Maybe some stuck around all year and she never noticed.

Essie waited a moment before turning back around and picking up her pace. The muscles in her arms were burning from carrying the luggage and the backpack. She couldn't wait to get to the pavement where she could wheel the two suitcases.

Crunch!

She whipped around again. Still didn't see anything. But it was a long and winding driveway. Someone or something could be just around the bend, and probably was from the sound of it.

It was likely only a forest critter. A raccoon scavenging for its next meal, most likely.

Essie started walking again, beads of sweat forming on her forehead. She really hadn't thought this through. The smart thing would've been to call for a ride. Since she'd taken money for the bus ride, it would have been just as easy to do that.

Crunch!

"Essie!"

She froze mid-step. Noah had found her.

"What are you doing?" he asked.

More gravel crunched as he made his way to her.

If she didn't have all those bags, she'd have run. Didn't he read the letter? Or did he not understand what she'd communicated so clearly?

He caught up to her and stood in front of her, gasping for air. "What are you doing?"

She couldn't look at him. Or hold the luggage any longer. She set it all down. "Didn't you find my note?"

"Yes. Why are you doing this?"

"I explained everything in the letter." Her voice wavered. She cleared her throat and prayed for the strength to be able to say what she needed to in person. "It was wrong of me to lead you on as I did. For that, I'm sorry. I got swept away in my emotions, not that it's an excuse. I really do care for you."

He lightly touched her chin and guided it until she was looking at him. "Then why leave?"

"Don't you get it?" She blinked back tears.

"You want to go on mission trips."

"Exactly."

"But what does that have to do with us? Why break up with me again?"

Essie looked away. "It's like I explained, as much as I would love it, I can't have both. We can't. Our dreams aren't compatible."

"Why not?"

She snapped her attention to him. "What?"

"Do you think I have something against serving the poor?"

"No."

"Traveling?"

"No," she repeated. "But I will never be satisfied with week-long trips like most people. Everyone else who was going on the trip to Guatemala with me was going to leave after a week. I was the only one adopting and staying for years."

His expression was unreadable. "Have you ever *asked* me how I feel about long-term missions?"

She opened her mouth and then closed it. "I haven't."

"Then what makes you think you know how I feel about them?"

"You have all of this." She gestured up the driveway toward the house. "Plus Abby. She's in school. We couldn't leave for long periods of time."

"Why not? Your parents made it work with *three* kids. And we still managed to meet and fall in love."

She hesitated. "*Would* you want to move to Guatemala for five years? Or some other place? What if I ended up going into a country opposed to Christianity? It would be dangerous."

Noah cupped her chin and held her gaze.

It was a struggle not to get lost in his eyes.

"Es, I would follow you to the ends of the earth. I know what life is like without you, and I don't want that."

"But what I want isn't a vacation. It's a lifestyle, and sometimes a hard one. One time, my family and I didn't have access to a toilet for a full year."

"I understand, but I still think we can make it work."

"It's hardly something to compromise on!"

Hurt shone in his eyes. "Why are you trying so hard to push me away?"

"I'm not."

"Aren't you?"

She took a deep breath. "Our lives are so different."

"Doesn't mean it has to stay that way."

"What do *you* want?" Essie took a step back.

"You. All I want is you."

"What about Abby? You have to think about her. She won't want to be uprooted from her life."

Noah raked his fingers through his hair. "I always think about her. And time in the mission field would be good for her. If she turns out anything like you, then Adam and Cora would be proud."

"But she's in school."

"It's a Christian one, and they happen to hold spots for children of missionaries. Plus, from everything you've told me, education is still possible on the field. When you started high school halfway through, you were smarter than anyone else."

Her face warmed. "I was not."

"Sure you were." He stepped closer and laced his fingers through hers. "I'm not sure if you're scared or if you're really worried about our dreams not meshing, but you have nothing to worry about. I *want* to go where you go, and more than that, I've been given the means to help us get there. And about the house, I can hire someone to keep an eye on things."

Her heart fluttered and hope rooted inside. Was it actually possible they could make things work between them?

Noah squeezed her hands. "And another thing to consider, our town is a mission field. Gone are the days when most people went to church on Sunday. Have you noticed all the empty buildings? The demolished ones? Many people right here need to hear the good news for the first time."

"That's true. But..."

"But what?"

"It feels like taking the easy way out."

"Why? You don't have to travel to another country to find needs. We could volunteer at a soup kitchen or even start a ministry of our own. That would be fun, don't you think?"

"What kind of ministry?"

"I'm not sure, but I'm positive we can come up with some way to help the poor."

A warmth spread through her, both for him and also the idea of being able to make a difference locally.

"What do you think?"

"I do like the idea of finding a need around here and meeting it."

He wrapped his arms around her. "I can't tell you how happy that makes me."

"But what about Daniela?"

"Let's pick her up and bring her back here. We can bring some supplies for the orphanage and stay for a while. I could offer to put my handyman skills to work and you could spend some time doing what you were planning originally."

Tears blurred her vision. "Do you really mean it?"

"No, I'm making it all up."

Her mouth fell open.

Noah laughed. "I'm kidding. Of course I mean it. I want to be with you, and I want you to have your dreams come true. That is, if you don't mind me being part of your plans."

"Are you joking? That would be the best of both worlds."

"You're sure?"

"Yes! Why do you keep asking?"

He licked his lips, his expression becoming unreadable again. "I needed to be certain." Then he reached into an inside pocket of his jacket and fidgeted before pulling out his fist.

"Certain of what?"

Noah cleared his throat and lowered down to one knee.

She stared in disbelief, her heart thundering.

He held her left hand in his. "I've wanted to marry you for as long as I can remember. Since long before I proposed before, and certainly every moment since then—even if I wasn't fully aware of it. Es, you're the most amazing woman I've ever met, and you inspire me to be the best man I can be. It would be a huge honor if you would agree to become my wife. I promise you it isn't something I'll take lightly, and I will do my level best to think of your needs above my own and to be the best husband I can for you. Will you marry me?"

It took her a moment to find her voice. "Yes! I don't know why I've fought against this so much, but nothing would make me happier. I love you, Noah."

He rose to his feet and kissed her before sliding the ring onto her finger.

It fit perfectly.

She moved her hand around to see it from every angle. "Is that the same one from before?"

"It is. I never could bring myself to return it. In a way, I think I always had an inkling of hope that we could work things out some day."

"I'm so glad you never gave up on me."

"Me too." He embraced her and spun her in a circle before setting her down. "Why don't we get this luggage back to the guesthouse so you can settle back in?"

Essie beamed, hardly able to believe any of this was real. She'd packed her bags never expecting to see him.

Now they were going to get married.

CHAPTER 17

Noah cleared his throat as he tugged on his tie. The sanctuary was filled more than he'd expected. Especially considering how little notice the guests had been given and that Christmas was only days away.

Once Essie had agreed to marry him, she didn't want to wait. He didn't object—not considering how long he'd been waiting for this moment.

The sanctuary was already decorated with wreaths, garland, and simple white lights. It was perfect, and they had opted not to change a thing for their ceremony.

At the moment, it was only the pastor and him at the front of the room. Soon Essie would join them.

Time had never dragged so slowly.

He couldn't wait to see her. She had made such a big deal about this being a small gathering and her dress not being fancy, but he knew she would be beautiful no matter what she wore.

He smiled at people in attendance. Scarlett and her family. Other family members. Friends from church. Colleagues. Old friends from high school and college who remembered Noah and Essie dating the first time around. A few people he didn't recognize—people Essie had befriended over the years, no doubt.

If only their parents and siblings could be there. His would never return, but at least they could celebrate with hers when they returned to town. What a surprise this would be!

His best friend Jack entered and closed the doors. He turned and gave a wide grin to Noah.

Soft instrumental music played over the speakers. A couple from Essie's church stepped up to microphones off to the side and sang a soft melody, growing louder with each line.

Noah's heart leaped into his throat.

His fiancée would soon walk through those doors.

Jack opened them, and a moment later Abby bounced into the room smiling in a pretty white dress. She practically skipped down the aisle, dropping rose petals along the way. Then she stepped onto the platform next to Noah, clutching her basket.

Everyone seated rose.

Then Essie appeared in the doorway.

Noah's breath caught. Nobody had ever looked so beautiful. She was right about the dress being simple compared to how extravagant most people went these days. But it was still elegant and she made it shine.

Her eyes widened for a moment—she was probably as surprised as him at how many people took the time out for a wedding so close to Christmas—then she glanced his way and grinned.

It seemed to take forever for her to reach the front. Maybe every groom felt that way.

She finally stood in front of him, and everything else disappeared. This was actually happening. They were getting married. By the time they stepped back onto the aisle, she would be his wife.

A true Christmas miracle.

Noah could hardly focus on anything the pastor said. Somehow, he managed to follow directions as they lit the unity candle and recited the traditional vows before exchanging the rings Abby had held on to for them.

Then came the magical moment.

His pastor beamed, looking back and forth between Noah and Essie. "Before God and these witnesses, I declare you husband and wife. You may kiss the bride."

Noah's heart thundered as he lifted the veil and took in the sight of his beautiful bride. He pressed his lips on hers, letting the kiss linger long enough to still be chaste in front of the guests.

Abby jumped up and down. "You're married! You're married!"

Most everyone laughed.

Then as soon as Noah and Essie turned toward the steps to walk off the platform, the guests broke out in applause.

Hand in hand, they made their way down the aisle.

Once outside the fellowship hall, he turned to her. "I can't believe you're my wife."

"And I couldn't be any happier."

He gave her one more kiss before the guests rounded the corner to celebrate with them.

CHAPTER 18

❄

Essie sipped her peppermint cocoa and smiled at Noah as he helped Abby assemble a miniature barn.

Everything still felt like a dream. It was hard to believe she and Noah were actually married, but they were. She no longer lived in the guesthouse, but the main house.

Abby had welcomed her with open arms, thrilled with the marriage. Essie had been a little nervous about that. Even though Abby had been excited about Essie moving into the guesthouse, the permanency of marriage could've soiled her feelings. But they hadn't. The little girl was thrilled about being part of a family again.

Noah rose and dusted off his hands. "Who's ready for lunch?"

Abby didn't even look up from her toy horses.

Essie reached for his hand. "I'm more than ready since we skipped breakfast."

He kissed her. "Let me check on the turkey. We—wait. What's that?"

"What?" Essie looked around, confused.

"That." He pointed to the tree.

"A tree?"

"Underneath."

It was empty. She turned to him. "What do you mean?"

"We missed a present."

She knelt for a closer look. Still nothing. "Do you need to get your eyes checked?"

The corners of his mouth wobbled. He leaned down, and as he did, reached into the pocket of his robe.

What was he doing? He'd already proposed. They were married. What other surprise could he be hiding?

"Look. We did miss one." He whipped out an envelope.

She tilted her head, studying him.

He handed it to her. "Open it."

Essie stared at it.

"It won't bite." He chuckled.

"We'll see." She slid her finger underneath and opened the seal. Pulled out the folded papers. Looked at them, but still didn't understand. "What's this?"

He beamed. "Tickets to Guatemala. Three there and four returning. I spoke with Sarah and worked out all the details. Tomorrow we leave to pick up Daniela, and we'll stay in a spare room in the orphanage. For two weeks we'll help them out with whatever they need. It sounds like mostly painting, but some other small jobs too."

Essie could hardly believe it. They were leaving the next day to pick up Daniela. She threw her arms around him and squeezed as hard as she could. "Thank you!"

He coughed. "Can't breathe!"

She loosened her grip.

Abby ran over and joined the embrace. "I'm really going to be a big sister?"

"Yes." Essie couldn't wipe the grin off her face. "Let me show you Daniela's picture." She scrolled through the images on her phone and stopped at the first one of the little girl.

"I can't wait to meet her!" Abby jumped up and down.

"She only speaks a few words of English. It'll be a while before she understands us and can speak the language."

"I know some Spanish." Abby nodded enthusiastically. "I learned it in school."

Essie hugged her. "I've been studying the language myself. Hopefully, between the two of us we can understand most of what she says."

Abby danced around the room singing about becoming a sister.

Noah pulled her close. "Merry Christmas."

"Thank you for making all my dreams come true. I didn't realize it until you proposed, but marrying you is exactly what I didn't know I wanted."

He kissed her. "And I couldn't be happier about that."

THANK you for reading *Yours for Christmas*. I hope you enjoyed it. If you'd like to read my upcoming books, please sign up here for updates: https://www.subscribepage.com/addisonblaire

Turn the page to find out more about my next book, *Always You…*

COMING SOON

ALWAYS YOU

Pre-order *Always You* today!

Gretchen has always tried to do the right thing, but now she wonders if any of her good deeds made a difference. Between her canceled wedding, her boss firing her, and the eviction notice, she's certain it's time to crawl back under the covers and let the world sort itself out.

Instead, she holds her head high and returns to her hometown to live with her parents, where she attempts to mend her broken heart and bruised faith. Life settles into a pleasantly boring normalcy she didn't know she'd missed. Until she sees Brant—her childhood best friend that she always had a secret crush on.

When recently widowed Brant runs into Gretchen at a local party, he can't believe his eyes. He hasn't seen her since she fled town after their high school graduation. With their mutually broken hearts, they fall back into an easy friendship.

This time, something more sparks. As they start to open their hearts, they realize God might have a plan for them—together.

But are they ready to accept it?